Almost Goodbye Guzzler

Helen Cresswell and Judy Brown

Collins

Look out for more *Jets* from Collins

Jessy Runs Away • *Best Friends* • **Rachel Anderson**
Ivana the Inventor • *Ernest the Heroic Lion Tamer* • **Damon Burnard**
Two Hoots • *Almost Goodbye Guzzler* • **Helen Cresswell**
Shadows on the Barn • **Sarah Garland**
Nora Bone • *The Mystery of Lydia Dustbin's Diamonds* • **Brough Girling**
Thing on Two Legs • *Thing in a Box* • **Diana Hendry**
Desperate for a Dog • *More Dog Trouble* • **Rose Impey**
Georgie and the Dragon • *Georgie and the Planet Raider* • **Julia Jarman**
Cowardy Cowardy Cutlass • *Free With Every Pack* • **Robin Kingsland**
Mossop's Last Chance • *Mum's the Word* • **Michael Morpurgo**
Hiccup Harry • *Harry Moves House* • **Chris Powling**
Rattle and Hum, Robot Detectives • **Frank Rodgers**
Our Toilet's Haunted • **John Talbot**
Rhyming Russell • *Messages* • **Pat Thomson**
Monty the Dog Who Wears Glasses • *Monty's Ups and Downs* • **Colin West**
Ging Gang Goolie, it's an Alien • *Stone the Crows, it's a Vacuum Cleaner* •
Bob Wilson

First published by A & C Black Ltd in 1990
Published by Collins in 1990
10 9 8 7 6 5
Collins is an imprint of HarperCollins*Publishers*Ltd,
77–85 Fulham Palace Road Hammersmith, London W6 8JB

ISBN 0 00 673881 8

Text © Helen Cresswell 1990
Illustrations © Judy Brown 1990

The author and the illustrator assert the moral right to
be identified as the author and the illustrator of the work.
A CIP record for this title is available from the British Library.

Printed and bound in Great Britain by
    Omnia Books Ltd, Glasgow

Susie Potts and Guzzler Gummidge
were best friends.

So were their mothers,

4

Mrs Potts and Mrs Gummidge went on about this so much, it was a wonder Susie and Guzzler weren't worst enemies.

Susie and Guzzler were in Class 4
at Witherspoon Road Junior School.

Their teacher was Miss Toasty.
She was very very very very boring.

So Susie and Guzzler sat at the back of the class and did their own thing.

They played noughts and crosses, mostly.

Or hangman.

Or consequences.

Miss Toasty met...

Batman

In the ladies lav

She said 'Do you like my whiskers'.

He said with salt + vinegar

What she did: She sneezed six billion 467 timez

What he did: He chewed a ratburger

The conzekwences: a shark et them and got indergeschun

They fell about giggling and ate a lot of crisps.

Miss Toasty droned on and on and on.

One day Miss Toasty rapped on her desk with her ruler.
The class looked up – even Susie and Guzzler.
'I have some very exciting news!' she said.

'A White Elephant is something that you no longer want,' Miss Toasty went on. 'But it may be exactly what someone else is looking for.'

I want you all to ask at home

said
Miss Toasty.
'And then you
can also go round
knocking at doors.
You must be very polite, and you
must work in pairs.'

'Bags Guzzler and me!' yelled Suzy.

'I think,' said Miss Toasty 'that
some people at the back are
being silly.'

THE GREAT KNOCK BEGAN . . .

Class 4 of Witherspoon Road Junior
School went banging on doors and
ringing bells.
Abdul Singh and Julie Boot were in
charge of the wheelbarrow.

Up and down the streets they
charged with it.
Into it went . . .

hamsters' cages . . .

leaking cushions...

jigsaws with half the pieces missing...

babies' rattles with no rattle....

broken toasters...

YOU NAME IT!!

Miss Toasty was delighted.
You could tell this by the way she
clapped her hands.

Splendid!
Keep it up!

Susie Potts and Guzzler Gummidge
went off on their own. They wanted
to collect umpteen white elephants
– more than the rest of the class put
together.

They decided to concentrate on
old people.
'I reckon the older you are, the more
white elephants you've got,'
said Susie.

(Susie and Guzzler's manners were quite good when they tried.)

Mrs Lane was certainly very old, and she lived on her own.
Inside it was quite dark. The walls were covered with pictures.
Everywhere was crowded with pots and knick-knacks. It looked to Susie and Guzzler as if Mrs Lane *lived* in a white elephant stall.

That's Ermintrude. Say hello nicely, Ermintrude!

Goodbye nicely! This is BBC Radio Four! Whoops a daisy!

A parrot!

Mrs Lane fetched some orange squash and a tin of biscuits. Needless to say these went down very well.

The biscuit tin emptied fast –
Guzzler Gummidge wasn't called
Guzzler for nothing.
Susie fed her biscuits to Ermintrude
because she liked to watch the
parrot's beak working. It seemed
to be on hinges.

Mrs Lane came back with her white elephant.

Now - what about this? It's very old

Looks like Aladdin's lamp to me

What is it?

I've got a loverly bunch of coconuts!

'I remember Alfred buying this from an antique shop when we were first married,' Mrs Lane told them. 'I'm afraid it's rather dusty. Everything's dusty. My old hands are rather shaky these days.'

'How very kind,' said Mrs Lane. 'Thank you.'

(I told you Susie and Guzzler had good manners. *And* hearts of gold.)

They thanked Mrs Lane, promised to see her next week to do the dusting, and went off with the lamp.

THE LAMP

Suzy and Guzzler went and sat in the park while they decided where to knock next. They stared at the one thing they had collected so far.

It was easy to see that *this* was a white elephant. What possible use could it be to anyone? And it certainly was dusty.

Guzzler gave it a rub.

Does look a bit like Aladdin's lamp!

Wish it was- with a real live genie!

25

Guzzler's mind was a total blank.

So was Susie's.

They were flabbergasted.

Poleaxed.

GOBSTRUCK.

They gaped up at the genie in his
swirl of blue and green smoke.
'I am the genie of the lamp. You have
two wishes left!' he said.
Two wishes? Could they both be
asleep and dreaming the same dream?

WISHES

You just don't go round expecting to have wishes granted. No one does. Perhaps we should all carry round a card with three wishes, like a donor card. Then we'd be ready for emergencies. As it was, Susie and Guzzler were caught on the hop.

The genie disappeared in a puff of smoke and a roar like a gas jet. Guzzler and Susie blinked. Had they imagined the whole thing?

29

Guzzler had gone.

His clothes were empty.

At first neither of them could take
it in.

Guzzler was exceedingly chuffed
to be invisible.

He meant to . . .

stick his tongue out
at Miss Toasty . . .

go through every door that said
NO ADMITTANCE . . .

and best of all . . .

Guzzler tore off. He meant to do
just that, straight away. Susie
went after him.

There was an old tramp shuffling
through the park.
He stared, he gaped, he boggled.

He'd seen plenty in his long life on
the road, but never anything like this.
Guzzler Gummidge was out of the
park and into the street.
After him went Susie Potts at a
fast lick.

She was wishing she had her camera with her. No one was ever going to believe this.

'There's one thing,' she thought, 'he can use the last wish to come visible again!'

BUT CAN HE ???...

The poor old tramp thought he'd better have a sit down after a shock like that. His legs were like jelly.

Moral

Don't Leave Litter
lying about and
don't Leave magic
Lamps ( )

[especially when
they give three
wishes and you've
already
used up two]

A pair of grubby sneakers, a pair of jeans and a tee shirt were moving fast up Witherspoon Road. Guzzler's legs might be invisible, but they still worked.

Chasing after them was Susie Potts, who by now had stitch. She had stitch so seriously she thought she might end up in hospital.

The insurance people'll never believe me!

STITCH

KEEP YOUR TOWN TIDY

So did some other people who caught sight of the headless, armless, legless Guzzler.

Guzzler raced on, hell-bent for the girl's toilets.

His mind was working fast.
He wondered if he really was like a ghost, and could go through things.
He decided to test it out on a lamp post.

Guzzler rubbed the invisible bump
on his invisible nose.
He wondered if he needed some
invisible sticking plaster.

At last Susie caught up.

'This is terrific,' Guzzler told her.
'Where's old Toasty?'

He certainly didn't.

said Susie, who was getting fed up.

That was when the

You'll have to take them OFF!

Guzzler stared with his invisible eyes.

WHAT?! And go round starkers? No fear!

...l truth dawned.

You've got it!

SHOCK HORROR!

The tramp had no idea what the lamp was for. He just hoped it would be worth a bob or two. He picked it up.

Susie thought fast. She saw the kids playing football.
'Quick – get behind that tree!' she told Guzzler. She went over to the kids.
'Hey – did you take a lamp off this seat?' she asked them.

Guzzler then made a

GREAT TACTICAL ERROR

he came out from behind the tree.
To be fair, he didn't exactly realize
what a fearsome spectacle he was.
'A tramp? Where did he go?'
he demanded. The kids went into a

MEGA PANIC

HELP!

It's a phantom
tee shirt!

RUN
FOR
IT !!

Susie and Guzzler were now in
a DIRE QUANDARY.

It looked as if a tramp had made off
with the lamp – *plus resident genie!*

And there was only one wish left!!!

Meanwhile the panic stricken kids had gone to dial 999.

Susie and Guzzler raced on.
Everything now depended on finding
that tramp before he made a wish.
By now Guzzler was beginning to
wish he had taken off his clothes.

At least he'd be totally invisible if
he were starkers.
He was attracting too much
attention for comfort.

The tramp went plodding on, quite unaware that he had a genie to command. He could have wished for a million pounds, if only he'd known it. He could have wished for a *zillion*.

He could have wished to sprout wings, or breathe fire.

Soon he was tired again, so he went and sat in a bus shelter.

Cor, my feet are killing me! Wish I'd got a- a...

...a...   ...a...   ...a...

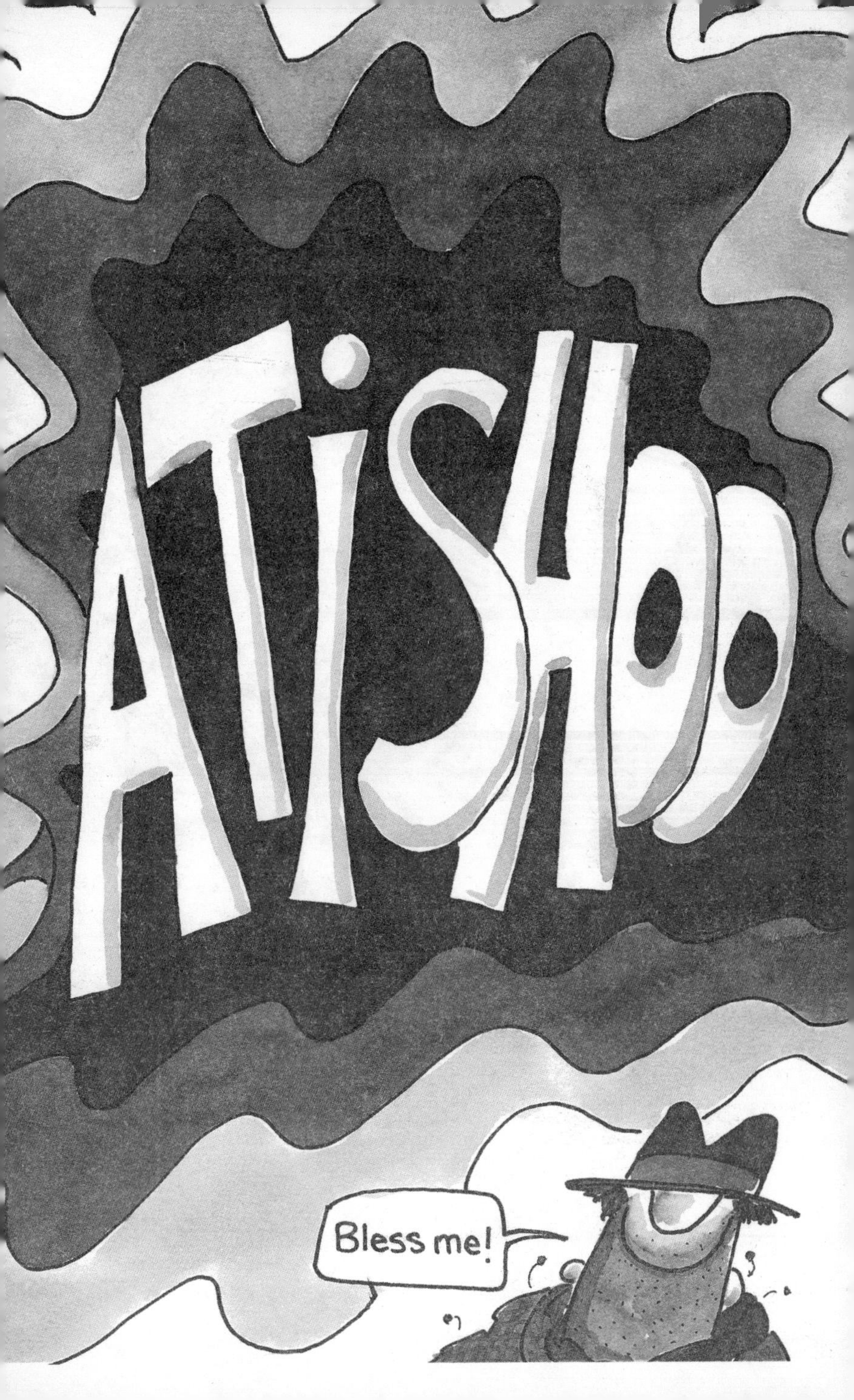
ATISHOO
Bless me!

By now the police were arriving on the scene. Their switch-board had been jammed with calls. They could not make head or tail of them, but thought they had better investigate anyway.

Never make a photofit of that!

Susie and Guzzler heard the police. It looked as if the game was up. They raced on – but too late, the police had spotted them.

Then, at the eleventh hour, Susie and Guzzler spotted the tramp ahead.

He was just going into the bus
shelter. They doubled their speed
until they were breaking Olympic
records.

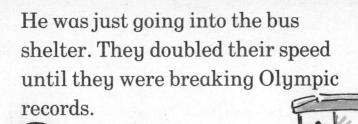

The police jumped out of their cars
and went after them, wondering
how to arrest a tee shirt, and what
they'd charge it with?

Before he could finish his sentence
Susie and Guzzler appeared on
the scene.
'There it is!' yelled Guzzler, and
grabbed the lamp.

But the tramp was too late.
He'd missed his chance. No million,
no zillion, no wings.
Nothing.

The police had a lot of trouble sorting out what had happened – or rather, *not* sorting it out, because they never did. Policemen can't go round believing in magic lamps and wishes. So in the end they decided to forget the whole thing and let everybody off with a caution.

The Bring and Buy at Witherspoon Road Junior School was a great success.

Susie and Guzzler handed the lamp over to Miss Toasty.

They were actually quite pleased to see the back of it. It never even occurred to them that the next person to have it would get three wishes too . . .

At the sale, Miss Toasty herself
bought the lamp for a pound.

Miss Toasty hurried off to put the
lamp in her desk, so that it
wouldn't be sold twice.
She didn't really trust Class 4 to
be sensible in her absence.

'Oh – it's at times like this' she said,
'I wish I had two pairs of hands' –